to Barbara Bottner

1

Who can it be?

To Whom It May Concern,
    If you liked this book, try Trapped in
the Asteroid Belt.   Your Cosmic Cousin

Emily Butler was sprawled on the
bottom bunk, halfway through *Terrors
of the Time Warp* when she found this
message. It was written on the back of a
bookmark.

'Alma, listen to this.' She read the
note out loud to her older sister in the
top bunk.

'Who do you think wrote this? Alma?
ALMA?'

Alma dragged her eyes away from her

own book, *Prom Night Promises*. 'Who wrote what?'

Emily read the note again.

'Let me see that.' Alma took the bookmark carefully so she wouldn't smear her nail polish. Their mother allowed them to use nail polish when they got to be thirteen, and Alma had wasted no time.

'*Trapped in the Asteroid Belt*.' Alma wrinkled her nose. 'Sounds like a terrible book. Here.'

Emily grabbed the bookmark back. It sounded like a wonderful book to her. She read the note again then turned it over. 'Hey! Cosmic Cousin must go to my school. This is one of the bookmarks we got on the first day of school. I wonder who it is.'

She studied the handwriting. She liked the way it looked.

Who could it be, she wondered. It

was exciting to find a message from someone who liked the same sort of books she liked. It was even more exciting to think that whoever it was went to her school and might be someone she knew. But who? How could she figure it out? The handwriting was her only clue. She knew she would recognize it if she saw it again.

The next day, Emily held her breath as she hunted through the shelves for *Trapped in the Asteroid Belt*. She found it at last and sat right down on the library steps to read the first chapter. After the first chapter, she went on to the second. Emily liked to read so much that once she started she had a hard time stopping. In the summer reading club at the library, she had read more books than anyone her age. Her spaceship had zoomed all the way to Pluto on the reading-club chart.

After chapter 5 she began to walk slowly, looking up from the book only when she reached street corners. She was almost at her front door when she found another bookmark and another note.

To Whom It May Concern,
 Invasion of the Pluto People is even better than this book. It's my favourite. I've read it twice already.　Your Cosmic Cousin

---

Emily raced back to the library. She flipped impatiently through the catalogue for the title and then searched the shelves. *Invasion of the Pluto People* was in. Her luck was holding. As she went to check it out, she wondered if there was a note in this one. That would be perfect. Another note and then another book and then another note . . .

8

QUIET
PLEASE

'EMILY BUTLER! What are you doing to that book? You'll break the spine shaking it like that,' said Mrs Rindfuss, the librarian.

'Sorry, Mrs Rindfuss.'

'And please try to take out *all* your books at one time,' Mrs Rindfuss said, firmly pressing her glasses to her nose.

Emily studied the picture on the cover and read a few pages before putting the new book into her backpack. *Invasion of the Pluto People* looked good but there was no note in it. At least, none had fallen out when she shook it. Had she come to the end of the notes already?

She glanced around the library as she backed out the door. Cosmic Cousin might be here at this very moment, looking like any other kid. Who could it be? Whoever it was, Cosmic Cousin had great taste in books.

That night, Emily had trouble deciding which new book to read. This was the kind of trouble she liked. She could finish *Trapped in the Asteroid Belt* since she only had four more chapters to go. Or she could start *Invasion of the Pluto People*. Finally, she settled on *Invasion of the Pluto People*. If this was Cosmic Cousin's favourite book she couldn't go wrong.

It *was* good – so good she finished it by torchlight, under the covers, even though it was hard to do because she had to hold the torch with her teeth when she turned the pages.

Up to the very end, she hoped to find another message from Cosmic Cousin – perhaps scribbled in the margin – but there was none. Emily was depressed. At last she fell asleep with her head under the covers.

2

Solar Soulmate

The next morning, Emily woke up early. Her head was still under the covers, and her ear was jammed against the torch.

She lay in bed, rubbing her sore ear and thinking about the notes from Cosmic Cousin. Finally she got out of bed to find her backpack. The two notes were in there, tucked in the secret compartment of her pencil box. She read the first note. It told her nothing new. Then, as she was reading the second note, she had a great idea. *Invasion of the Pluto People* was Cosmic Cousin's favourite book – good enough to read twice. There was just a chance Cosmic Cousin would read it again.

Emily sometimes did that with books she liked. She decided to write her own note.

Dear Cosmic Cousin,

I really liked this book! Have you read <u>Aliens I Have Known</u>? It's almost always out, so if I find it for you, I'll put it under the library table by the window.

Your Solar Soulmate

P.S. There's a ledge under the table.

Emily opened *Invasion of the Pluto People* and wedged her note as tightly as possible into the binding. After school that day, she took it back to the library.

Then she looked for *Aliens I Have Known*. For once, the book was in. She thought this was a good sign her plan would work. Checking to see that no one was watching, she hid the book on the ledge under the table by the window. There. Now all she had to do was wait for Cosmic Cousin to re-read the book, find her note, and look under the table.

But Emily was not very good at waiting. She checked under the table after school every day for a week. *Aliens I Have Known* was still hidden there. She also looked to see if *Invasion of the Pluto People* had been taken out. No luck. It was still on the shelf.

One week went by. When Emily was

at the library, instead of paying attention to her work she studied the other kids, trying to figure out which one was her mysterious pen pal. It could be anyone. Remembering the bookmark, she kept her eye on the kids from her school. A lot of them took the bus to the library after school and hung around for a while. Some of them did homework or got out books to read – especially when Mrs Rindfuss was watching – and some of them just talked.

Emily decided to start first with the kids who came to the library a lot.

Walter Kenney was usually there. He must have sensed Emily staring at him because he looked up and smiled. Embarrassed, she smiled back and then quickly looked the other way.

Rachel Poindexter and Janie Hines were at the next table, talking and

giggling. Rachel was talking, as usual,
and Janie was giggling. The new kid,

Mary Louise Butterman, was studying
quietly beside them.

Then there was Eddie Mumford,
reading and chewing gum. The faster
he read, the faster his jaws moved.

Emily watched Eddie and wondered what he was reading.

Stanley Ferguson was sitting across from Eddie. Emily didn't have to wonder what he was reading. It *had* to be a book about dinosaurs. He was wearing his sweatshirt with the stegosaurus on the back.

Later, on her way to the drinking fountain, she saw her neighbour, Marcie Hubble, checking out books. She was with Joey Gebhart. Joey didn't have many books but they were very thick. They looked interesting. But Emily couldn't get close enough to read the titles.

By the beginning of the next week, Emily was getting desperate. Maybe Cosmic Cousin would *never* find her note.

Then she discovered *Invasion of the Pluto People* wasn't on the shelf any more. Cosmic Cousin might have taken it out to re-read it.

Emily kept her fingers crossed every time she checked the table. Two days later, as she slid her hand over the book on the ledge, she thought it felt different from *Aliens I Have Known*. This was a thicker book. She pulled it out to take a peek. It was a book she'd never seen before – *The Return of the Martian Zyvitch* – and there was a note in it:

Dear Solar Soulmate,
　　Leaving books under the table is a great idea. You'll like this book. Chapter 7 is fantastic!　Your Cosmic Cousin

---

Emily could hardly believe it! Cosmic Cousin had found her note and had actually written back! Now that this plan had worked, Emily was sure she could find out Cosmic Cousin's identity. It would be exciting to follow clues and figure it out for herself. Someday soon she'd be able to say 'Hello, Cosmic Cousin,' and watch the look of surprise as they greeted each other.

Holding her new book tightly, Emily went to look for *Orbiting the Planet of Doom*. That was the next book she wanted to leave for Cosmic Cousin. Her heart was singing as she tucked it on to the ledge under the table.

3

The Zyvitch Test

Her best friend, Arnold Cosgrove, came by while Emily was sitting on her front steps reading *The Return of the Martian Zyvitch*. Arnold lived three houses down the street and was in her class at school. In fact, he sat next to her. Today he was looking even happier than usual.

'Have you read these yet?' He handed Emily two *Unknown Galaxy* comic books.

'Hey, thanks, Arnold! I've never read these. Where did you get them?'

'I swapped five of my old *Curse of the Vampire* comic books for them,' Arnold said, wiggling his ears. He had just discovered he could do this, and he liked to keep in practice.

Emily was pleased. *Unknown Galaxy* comic books were her favourites, and she knew Arnold had got them just for her. Any other time she would have started in on them immediately, but right now she was anxious to get on to chapter 7 of *The Return of the Martian Zyvitch*.

'You should read this, Arnold.' Emily showed him the cover of her book. He didn't seem interested.

'Oh, I don't know. It looks like a long book,' Arnold said. He had a pencil tucked above one ear and was trying to wiggle it loose.

'It's not that long. Just listen to the plot. There's a Zyvitch – that's a sort of space witch – and she rides around in a black hole trying to syphon sunshine from all the planets.' Emily gave him a

The Return of the Martian ZYVITCH

summary as far as chapter 6. 'It would make a great comic book,' she added.

Now Arnold looked interested. He liked to read comic books, but he liked to make up his own even more. Arnold was the best artist in the class. It was fun to sit next to him, reading the funny notes he gave her when their teacher wasn't looking.

'Is that the book you're giving your report on tomorrow?' Arnold asked.

'No. I'm giving mine on *Terrors of the Time Warp*. This is a book someone sort of gave me.'

'Who gave it to you?' Arnold asked. 'It looks like a library book to me.'

Emily hesitated. Should she tell Arnold about Cosmic Cousin? It would be fun to tell. And maybe Arnold could help her figure out who it was. On the other hand. . .

'Hi. What are you two talking about? Is it a secret?'

Emily looked around quickly. She saw Marcie Hubble from next door. Marcie was in her class too.

'Oh, nothing much,' Emily said. She was glad she hadn't been telling Arnold about Cosmic Cousin. Now she realized she wanted to keep it to herself. She especially didn't want Marcie to find out about it. Marcie *loved* secrets. And she could make one out of anything. Her birthday had been a month ago but she still hadn't told Emily what her best present was. That was a secret. She wouldn't even tell Emily her middle name. That was a secret, too. But if Marcie thought Emily had a secret, she'd keep after her to tell. So Emily was relieved when Marcie started talking about Hallowe'en.

'What are you guys going to be?' Marcie asked. 'It's only two weeks away, you know. I can't decide whether to be a butterfly or a bag of jelly beans.'

'You're crazy!' Arnold laughed. 'How can you be a bag of jelly beans?'

'It's easy. You get one of those big, clear plastic bags, and you stuff it with little balloons. Then you step into it and tie it around your neck. And you put a label on the front – YUMMY JELLY

BEANS. What are you guys going to be?' Marcie asked again.

'I'm going to be a vampire bat,' Arnold said. He explained how he was going to attach the bat ears to his own and wiggle them. 'But I have to build up my ear muscles first,' he admitted.

'I want to be a UFO but I don't know how to make the costume,' Emily said.

Marcie sighed. 'I wanted to be a ladybird but that new kid is going to be one. She told me she already had the costume from last year.'

'You mean Mary Louise? So let old Cheesy Lou-weesy be a ladybird and you can be a bird lady. Or a bird man.' Arnold started jumping around, flapping his arms.

'That's not funny, Arnold.' Marcie glared at him. 'And stop calling her Cheesy Lou-weesy.'

'Oh, you always stick up for the underdog,' Emily said. 'Nobody likes her.'

'Well, I think she's nice. By the way,' Marcie said, changing the subject, 'I saw you at the library, Emily, but you didn't see me.' Marcie smiled as if she knew a secret and wouldn't tell. 'I was just returning my book.'

All at once Emily was curious. She had known Marcie since playgroup but she didn't know what kind of books Marcie liked to read. 'What's the name of your book?' she asked.

'You'll find out tomorrow when I give my book report.' Marcie smiled again.

'Well, I'm not all *that* interested, you know,' Emily said.

But she was. She wondered why Marcie had mentioned seeing her at the library. Could Marcie have noticed her reaching under the table for the book from Cosmic Cousin?

Could *Marcie* be Cosmic Cousin?

Emily hadn't thought of it before, but it was possible. After all, Marcie did go to her school, and Emily did see her at the library sometimes.

Emily quickly decided on a way to check out this new possibility. 'I've changed my mind about Hallowe'en,' she said. 'I think I'll go as a Martian Zyvitch.'

'Hey, that sounds good,' Arnold said.

'What's a Zyvitch?' Marcie asked.

Was she just pretending she didn't know? Emily watched Marcie carefully as she explained what a Zyvitch was, but she couldn't tell a thing from the look on Marcie's face. Knowing Marcie, even if she were Cosmic Cousin, she'd never give up her secret so easily.

'It's time for tea,' Emily's mother called.

'See you guys tomorrow,' Emily said. And maybe that's not all I'll see, she thought. The book reports might give her some more clues about Cosmic Cousin.

4

Clues in the Classroom

'Emily Butler, please write your book title on the board,' said Mrs Gillies.

As usual, Emily was the first to give her book report. Mrs Gillies liked to do everything in an orderly, alphabetical way. Emily wished a few *A* names would join the class so she wouldn't have to be first all year.

While Emily told the class about *Terrors of the Time Warp*, she looked around to see if anyone was especially interested. Everyone was interested, but it was an exciting book. When she got to the part about the space captain suddenly shrinking to the size of an atom, all eyes were on her. But she couldn't tell if two of those eyes were Cosmic Cousin's.

Mrs Gillies called on Mary Louise Butterman next. Mary Louise was Emily's study buddy. And all because of their last names. *B* for Butler. *B* for Butterman. *B* for boring. Emily wished she weren't stuck with Mary Louise.

Study buddies were Mrs Gillies's latest bright idea. You had to work together for the last fifteen minutes every day, and sometimes longer before a big test. Almost *anyone* would be more fun to work with than Mary Louise.

She seemed so quiet, it was hard to get a hello out of her. Why, if she hadn't moved to their school, Arnold would be Emily's study buddy. Butler and Cosgrove – now that would be fun.

'Speak up, Mary Louise. I can't hear you,' Mrs Gillies said.

'My report isn't finished yet,' Mary Louise said, a little louder.

Mrs Gillies sighed. 'Well then, we'll have to go on to Arnold.'

Arnold's book report was very short, but he stretched it out by drawing the characters' faces on the board. He even wiggled his ears once.

The book reports went on. Emily

32

paid close attention to all of them, looking for clues. But nothing was turning up. Stanley Ferguson had read a book on dinosaurs, naturally. Joey Gebhart had read a long book on the discovery of rubber and gave a long report.

Emily's spine was beginning to *feel* like rubber, and she was getting too sleepy to concentrate. She glanced over to see if Arnold was working on his new comic book, 'Mrs Sillies and the Monster Class'. He was. With his book-report folder propped up in front as a cover, he was drawing Mrs Sillies, who looked a lot like the bride of Frankenstein and a little like Mrs Gillies. Emily also recognized some of the monsters he was drawing. They looked like kids in the class.

Then Marcie went to the blackboard to write her book title. Emily

straightened up to get a good view of the board. Marcie wrote *A Home for Al*. That didn't sound like a good science-fiction title to Emily.

'Can anyone guess who Al is?' Marcie asked.

Emily raised her hand. 'Is Al short for Alien?' she asked, without much hope.

Some of the kids laughed.

'No, it's not,' Marcie said. 'Are there any more guesses? Well, Al is just the cutest little black and white alley cat.' She showed everyone his picture in the book.

Emily felt let down. Now she remembered Marcie was a pushover for animals, especially strays. But Marcie might still be Cosmic Cousin, even though her book report didn't prove it. Emily could just imagine Marcie secretly slipping a note into a book.

Mrs Gillies called on Eddie Mumford next. As he was writing his title on the board, Emily snapped to attention. There was something familiar about Eddie's handwriting. It looked like a cross between printing and script. It looked just like the handwriting on the bookmark notes.

'This book is about one of my favourite sports. . . ,' Eddie mumbled.

Mrs Gillies stopped him right there. 'Please get rid of your gum, Eddie, and start again.'

Emily was staring so hard at his handwriting that she almost forgot to listen to his report. When she finally tuned in to it, Eddie was saying that the American Indians were the first to play something or other – Emily wasn't sure what.

'Thank you, Eddie,' Mrs Gillies said when he was done. 'I'm sure we all know more about lacrosse now than we did before. The rest of you will give your reports tomorrow.'

Well, if Eddie were Cosmic Cousin, you certainly couldn't tell it from his book report, Emily thought. Of course she *could* just ask him straight out – but that would be too easy. She wanted to be able to say, 'Ah ha! So *you're* Cosmic Cousin.'

Emily decided to get a closer look at the books Eddie liked to read at the library.

Library Research

After school, Emily took the bus to the library. She returned a few books at the desk.

'Only three books, Emily? You must have a dozen more at home.' Mrs Rindfuss looked at Emily as if she had better produce those books instantly.

'But they're not due yet,' Emily said. Mrs Rindfuss sniffed and turned abruptly to the next person in line.

Emily was smiling as she walked away. It felt so good to have the last word. She looked around for Eddie Mumford. He was there, chewing gum as hard as ever. She decided to stop at the drinking fountain near his table.

She paused behind his chair. She could see he wasn't doing his homework.

'Hi, Eddie. What are you reading?' Emily asked.

Eddie snapped his gum at her in a friendly way and showed her the front of his book – *Dodge Ball Danny*. Issues of *Sports Illustrated* magazine were piled beside him.

Emily had to admit Eddie was looking less and less like a candidate for Cosmic Cousin. But as she was thinking this, she glanced at his spelling book. His name was written on the cover in what looked exactly like Cosmic Cousin's handwriting. She couldn't take him off the list yet.

She went to the table by the window, sat down, and checked the ledge under it for a new book. As she did, she looked to see if Eddie was watching. If he really were Cosmic Cousin, he would be interested in that table. There was no new book, and Eddie didn't seem to be paying attention to her or the table.

She tried to think about what she was reading, but her mind kept racing back to Cosmic Cousin's notes and Eddie's handwriting.

'I can see you've been turning down the pages of these books again.'

Emily looked up to see who Mrs Rindfuss was scolding.

'I've warned you about this before, Janie,' Mrs Rindfuss said. 'Now, I'm sure Rachel *always* uses a bookmark,' she continued as she checked Rachel's books.

Bookmarks again. Emily gave up trying to remember her maths homework and started to think about Rachel. So Rachel used bookmarks. She was one grade ahead of Emily but they'd always been friends. Rachel loved to talk and Emily loved to listen.

The more she thought, the more she liked the idea of Rachel as Cosmic Cousin. She was the one who had got Emily interested in outer space in the first place. Last year, Rachel had wanted to become an astronaut. She had told Emily all sorts of amazing facts about the universe. The rings of Saturn were actually particles of ice, Rachel had said. Emily liked to think about them whirling around out there in space.

This year, Rachel wanted to be a vet and told Emily amazing facts about animals instead. That's how Emily found out that dogs sweat through their feet and that only female mosquitoes bite.

There was an empty seat across from Emily. Maybe Rachel would sit there. Emily wanted to talk to her and also

take a look at her handwriting. She
could see Rachel heading towards her
table. Good. Just then, Mary Louise sat
down in the empty seat. Rotten luck,
Emily thought, but she said hello.

'Do you know what pages we were
supposed to do for Maths?' Emily
asked.

'Pages 42 to 60, I think,' Mary
Louise answered.

'Hey, Mary Louise,' Emily leaned across and whispered. 'Did you see what Eddie did with his gum when Mrs Gillies told him to get rid of it? She thought he threw it in the wastepaper basket but I saw him put it behind his ear.' Emily laughed. 'I'll bet it's still there.'

She thought she saw a tiny smile, but Mary Louise didn't look up. Oh, well, you just couldn't get anywhere with some people, Emily thought as she flipped through her Maths book to page 42.

With Cosmic Cousin on her mind, Emily just couldn't sit still. She decided to get another drink before she started her homework. If she took the long way around to the drinking fountain, past Rachel's table, she might be able to get a glimpse of Rachel's handwriting.

Rachel was talking and laughing with

Janie Hines but when she saw Emily, she motioned to her. 'Did you watch that TV show on insects last night?' Rachel whispered.

'No. Was it good?' Emily whispered back.

'It was great!' Rachel went on. She forgot to whisper now. 'The part about earwigs was really *amazing*. You wouldn't believe what a good mother an earwig is. Sit down and I'll tell you how they feed their babies . . .' Rachel paused to take a breath.

'Tell me tomorrow,' Emily whispered hastily. 'I'll meet you at break.' It was hard to stop Rachel once she started talking, and Emily could see Mrs Rindfuss frowning at them. She thought she had better move on. Before she left, she tried to get a look at Rachel's handwriting. But *The Big Book of Penguins* was covering her notebook.

Now it seemed to be animals, animals and more animals with Rachel. Still, Emily didn't think Rachel could have completely lost interest in outer space. How could anyone forget those ice rings of Saturn?

Emily decided to check out one more person before she sat down again. She looked around. Who would be next?

Walter Kenney was a possibility. He came to the library as often as she did, and he always took out lots of books. He went to her school – in fact, he was the friendliest boy there. Thinking about Walter, Emily began to get her hopes up.

She walked behind his chair and looked quickly to see what he was reading. At least she meant to do it quickly, but she couldn't stop reading.

'Jo! Jo! Where are you?' cried Meg, at the foot of the garret stairs.

'Here!' answered a husky voice from above. . . .

The names seemed very familiar. Emily realized she was reading *Little*

Women. That meant Walter was reading *Little Women*.

Walter looked up at her. He didn't have his usual friendly grin. He seemed embarrassed. 'I was just sort of looking through this book. My sister asked me to get it out for her.'

'Hey, it's a good book. Anybody would like it,' Emily said.

Walter glared at her. That hadn't been the right thing to say.

She tried again. 'I mean, your sister will really like it.' Walter still wasn't smiling.

Emily slunk back to her table. Well, Walter *had* been the friendliest boy in her school. Now he was going to think she was spying on him. This research business wasn't going very well. Maybe tomorrow there would be some good clues in the rest of the book reports.

Suddenly, she sneezed three times, very loud. Mrs Rindfuss, shelving books nearby, said 'Emily Butler, *where* is your handkerchief?'

6

List of Suspects

The next day, Emily stayed home with the flu.

'Keep away from my diary, Emily,' Alma warned her as she left to catch the bus. 'You can read my new book, though, if you want to.'

'*The Summer of Jennifer's Dreams*? I'd rather read Yellow Pages!' Emily yelled after her.

Emily's mother came in to check her temperature. 'If you feel too sick to read, you can lie on the couch and watch TV,' she said.

'No thanks, Mum, but I'd like a pack of cards and some ginger ale, please.'

All morning she played patience,

sipped ginger ale, and thought about Cosmic Cousin. She didn't want to be sick at home. There she couldn't pick up any more clues about Cosmic Cousin's identity.

Emily decided to write down a list of people who might be Cosmic Cousin. After some thought she narrowed it down to five names.

Rachel was first on the list because Emily thought that deep down Rachel must still have an interest in outer space. After all, some day there would be animals on space colonies. There'd be plenty of work for a vet out there.

Then again, it might be Eddie Mumford. He did *write* like Cosmic Cousin. Maybe he read sports books during the week and science fiction at the weekend.

Walter Kenney was next. She still liked that idea, although she had

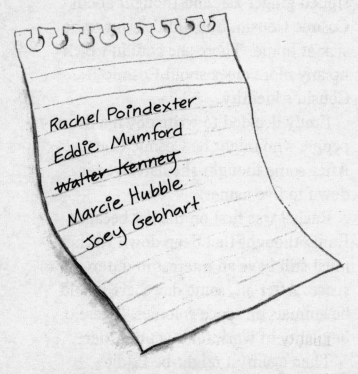

Rachel Poindexter
Eddie Mumford
~~Walter Kenney~~
Marcie Hubble
Joey Gebhart

nothing to go on. Regretfully, she crossed off his name.

She also put Marcie's name on her list, just because leaving secret notes in books was something Marcie would love to do.

Joey Gebhart was another possibility she'd had in the back of her mind. At the science fair last year, he had won first prize for their age group with his Morse code transmitter. Her imagination leaped ahead. Maybe this year they could work on a science-fair project together.

She crawled out of bed to get a tissue and to look for her book with the build-it-yourself-telescope plans. She could send away for the lenses if Joey would help pay for them. She moved Joey's name to the top of her list.

That was Wednesday.

By Thursday, Emily decided Rachel was a better possibility than anyone else. She remembered all those wonderful things that Rachel had told her last year about space.

By Friday morning, she favoured Eddie over the rest. After all,

handwriting never lies. She had read
that somewhere.

By Friday afternoon, Joey was back
in the lead. She had her heart set on the
telescope project.

On Friday evening, Marcie brought
Emily her homework.

'I have some bad news for you,'
Marcie said.

'What is it?' Emily asked uneasily.

'Mrs Gillies changed Arnold's seat.

Now he's up at the front so Mrs Gillies can keep an eye on him. That's what she said.'

'Oh no! What happened? Did she find the comic book he was working on?' Emily asked.

'Yep. That's what happened. She found "Mrs Sillies and the Monster Class". Arnold can really draw, can't he. Even Mrs Gillies admitted that,' Marcie said.

Emily sighed. She was going to miss watching Arnold at work.

'Who sits next to me now?' Emily asked.

'Stanley.'

'Oh no. Not Stegosaurus Stanley.' Emily sighed again. All she'd get to watch now would be dinosaur doodles.

Then, cheering up, she thought of a quick test to try on Marcie. Marcie was still on her Cosmic Cousin list – even though she was at the bottom.

'Marcie,' Emily began, 'why don't you dress up as a spy for Hallowe'en?' Marcie looked surprised but interested.

'You could dress in black and wear a false beard. . .' Marcie was looking doubtful now.

'Don't you think it would be fun to be a spy and sneak around leaving secret messages in all sorts of places –

like books?' This was daring. She
watched Marcie carefully.

'I don't think I'd like a beard,'
Marcie said. 'I'd much rather be a

ladybird. By the way, Emily, may I borrow your red tights for my costume?'

'Sure, but I thought you said Mary Louise was going to be a stupid old ladybird,' Emily said, feeling cross, even though she hadn't really wanted Marcie to be Cosmic Cousin.

'I was wrong about that. I think she's going to be a fairy princess. I saw part of her costume and it's very pretty. All sparkly.' Marcie had been rummaging through Emily's chest of drawers while she talked. Now she held up the red tights and made a face when she saw the hole in the toe of the left foot. 'Thanks for the tights,' Marcie said as she left.

Emily pulled out her list and firmly crossed off Marcie's name.

Cosmos, Oklahoma

By the time Emily went back to school, she had worked out a new plan to discover Cosmic Cousin's identity. She got the idea from *Intergalactic Mutiny* and the way Captain Robodek figured out who the real alien was.

She managed to get behind Joey Gebhart in the dinner queue, and soon they were talking about the science fair. He wouldn't say much about his project, just hinted that it was pretty advanced.

'My cousin does a lot of interesting experiments like that,' Emily said, putting her plan into operation. 'Too bad he doesn't live around here. He lives in *Cosmos*, Oklahoma.'

Joey looked a little bored.

'I call him my *Cosmic Cousin*,' Emily added hopefully.

Joey moved ahead to pick up his beefburger.

Oh well, there went the build-it-yourself telescope project.

After lunch, Emily daydreamed through French. She missed having

Arnold in the seat next to her and wondered if he was working on a new comic book. Probably not. Mrs Gillies was still keeping a very close eye on him.

Toward the end of the day, Emily was ready for another try at uncovering Cosmic Cousin. After the bell rang, she saw Rachel walking out to wait for the school bus. Emily grabbed her backpack and ran down the hall after her.

'Where have you been lately?' Rachel asked when she saw Emily.

'I was sick last week,' Emily answered and then, to start a conversation, she said, 'You were going to tell me about the mother earwigs – remember?'

While Rachel talked, Emily tried to figure out how to work in her Cosmos, Oklahoma, question.

'Animals are really amazing, aren't they?' Rachel said when she had finished. 'I'm glad I've decided to be a vet.'

Now was her chance. 'That reminds me – I have a cousin who's studying to be a vet,' Emily said.

Rachel looked interested.

'She lives in *Cosmos*, Oklahoma.' Rachel looked positively excited now. Emily's hopes soared. 'I call her my Cosmic Cousin.' Rachel was about to say something. Just then the bus came.

'I'll save you a seat,' Emily called back to Rachel as she got on the bus. She was glowing inside. Her plan had worked. She had discovered who Cosmic Cousin was! Captain Robodek himself couldn't have done better. As soon as the kids on the bus quieted down, she could talk to Cosmic Cousin at last.

Emily was just ready to reveal that she was Solar Soulmate when Rachel asked her, 'What did you say you call your cousin? How soon is she coming to visit you?'

'What . . . ? Oh, I don't know.' Emily's hopes plunged back to the ground.

'I've got all sorts of questions to ask her,' Rachel went on. 'Where does she go to college? In Oklahoma? That's not too far from here. You could ask her to come to see you some time.'

Emily was too depressed to answer. Finally Rachel lost interest and moved on to other subjects.

'Did I tell you I pulled one of my goldfish through tail rot?' Rachel asked. 'I had to sit up all night, nearly, and change the water every fifteen minutes. I think that's what saved him.' Rachel paused thoughtfully. 'But the other three died.'

Rachel talked on but it was hard for Emily to pay attention. She wished the bus would get to the library soon.

In her mind, she went over the list again. She knew now that it wasn't Rachel or Joey. She had crossed Marcie off her list, and it probably wasn't Eddie. Who did that leave?

Only everybody else at the library!

8

A Last-Ditch Effort

When the bus reached the library, Rachel and Emily got off. Because Emily had been sick her books were overdue. As she was returning them and adding up the fines, Mrs Rindfuss seemed pleased.

'That will be seventy-five cents. I thought you were taking out too many books. What's this I find in your book, Emily Butler? A *used* tissue?'

'No, Mrs Rindfuss. It's clean.' Emily snatched it back.

Before beginning her homework, Emily browsed through the shelves looking for more books to take out. She also looked for *Intergalactic Mutiny* and found it. This was the next book she

wanted to leave for Cosmic Cousin.
Then she started for the table by the
window.

   She hurried when she saw someone
heading toward her usual seat. Since
she hadn't been to the library in nearly
a week, someone else might have got in
the habit of sitting there.

Emily reached the table first and sat down with relief. Now there should be a book waiting for her. She checked the ledge cautiously with her hand. She could feel a book, but it might be the one she had left for Cosmic Cousin a week ago. Making sure no one was watching, she pulled out the book. Oh, good! It was one she had never read – *The Milky Way and Beyond*. There was a note in it.

Dear Solar Soulmate,

I just finished this book. The first part is a little boring but keep going — the ending is great! Your Cosmic Cousin

---

Emily felt a little disappointed. She had sort of been hoping that the next note would be signed with a real name. At first it had been fun to track down clues, but now she just wanted to meet

Cosmic Cousin. She wanted to talk to
Cosmic Cousin.

Emily thought of all the things they
could do together.

They could camp out in the garden
and make a map of the constellations.
Emily had started one, but it would be
more fun to do with somebody.

They could play Emily's new
Andromeda Galactic Maze game.

And maybe Cosmic Cousin would
help her finish her UFO costume for
Hallowe'en.

Emily thought about how to find out
Cosmic Cousin's name. Maybe she
should give in and just ask in her next
note. It would be so much easier. . .
She thought about it some more.

But no, it wouldn't be as exciting as
figuring it out for herself. She would
just have to come up with some way to
find out who it was.

Before starting to make a new plan,
Emily wrote a note to put into
Intergalactic Mutiny.

Dear Cosmic Cousin,
   You're going to love this book. And I'll bet
you'll never guess who the real alien is.
                    Your Solar Soulmate
P.S. Captain Robodek is my all-time
favourite character.

She slipped the book under the table
and then concentrated on making her
plan. She went over several possibilities
before she settled on one. This plan had
a couple of drawbacks. She would have
to tell a lie, and that bothered Emily.
She decided to think of it as a cover
story – like the ones spies and detectives
use. The other drawback was whom she
had to tell this lie to. Mrs Rindfuss.
There was no getting around that one.

Emily took some money out of her backpack and went to the desk. She could feel her knees shaking.

'Mrs Rindfuss.'

'Just *one* moment. Can't you see that I'm busy?'

Emily waited. She felt more nervous than ever.

Finally, Mrs Rindfuss eyed Emily over the top of her glasses. 'Now what is it you want?'

'I just found a dollar bill in this book.' Emily held up the new book from Cosmic Cousin. 'Someone must have used it as a bookmark.

'That was very careless of someone, wasn't it?' Mrs Rindfuss said.

'I thought maybe you could look up the person who took this book out last. Then you could tell me who it was and I – '

Mrs Rindfuss cut in. 'I simply do not

have the time right now to look up
something like that.'

Emily turned away, putting the dollar
in her pocket. With anyone else but old
Rindfuss this plan would have worked.

'However – '

Emily turned around quickly.

'– you may leave the dollar with me and later I will look up the rightful owner.' Mrs Rindfuss stretched out her hand.

Oh no! Emily thought fast. 'Nooo. I guess I'll just keep it until someone asks you for it.'

'Very well, Emily. As you wish.'

Whew! That was close. She had nearly lost her dinner money for the next day.

Now that this plan had failed, Emily felt she had come to the end of the line.

9

All is Discovered

Emily pushed the dollar farther into her pocket as she walked back to the table by the window. She didn't look up until she was there. Then she saw that Gary Willets was sitting in her seat. He hadn't paid any attention to Emily's books or her backpack hanging on the chair. She picked up her books and unhooked her backpack. Gary looked up but didn't offer to move. It was a good thing she had already found the new book from Cosmic Cousin and left one in its place.

She sat down at the next table. The library was more crowded and noisier than usual. Some of the younger kids were really mucking about, drumming their pencils on the tables and throwing erasers.

Mrs Rindfuss rapped on her desk several times and then came over to their tables. 'Stop this racket immediately or you will all have to leave.' She glared around at everyone and went back to her desk.

Things were quieter for a few minutes and then one of the younger kids threw a paper aeroplane at Gary. It bounced off his head and landed on the floor beside his chair. Emily felt uneasy as she watched Gary bend over to pick it up. She suddenly wondered if she had shoved the book as far back as usual on the ledge.

'What's this?' she heard him say. Then he shouted, 'Hey! Look what I found!'

As he straightened up, she saw he was holding *Intergalactic Mutiny*. He was waving it around. Emily was frantic that her note might fall out.

'Gary Willets, if you persist in this behaviour, I shall have to ask you to leave,' Mrs Rindfuss said.

Just her luck. Any other day, Gary wouldn't have made such a big fuss. Any other day, Mrs Rindfuss wouldn't have been at his side like a shot.

'I was just saying that I found this book under the table,' Gary mumbled. 'On a ledge down here – see?'

Mrs Rindfuss stooped down to examine the ledge. She ran her finger over the book as if to check for dust.

'The very idea of *hiding* books at a public library. Now who would do a thing like that?' She narrowed her eyes at Gary.

'I didn't do it,' Gary protested. Suddenly he pointed at Emily and said,

'Why don't you ask her? She was sitting here before.'

It was very quiet now. Emily's heart had nearly stopped when Gary found the book, but now she thought everyone could hear it thudding. She wished *she* could crawl on to a ledge under the table.

'The rest of you boys and girls get back to work.' Mrs Rindfuss came over to Emily and in a lower voice asked, 'Emily Butler, do you know anything about this?'

'I wasn't sitting there very long,' Emily said, which was the truth – if not the whole truth.

Mrs Rindfuss looked suspiciously at Emily. Did she know Emily was lying – or nearly lying? Then she looked again at the book in her hand and said with surprise, 'Why, someone was asking for this very book just the other day.'

Mrs Rindfuss raised her voice again. 'I intend to find out who did this.' She swept the room with an angry look and marched away.

Oh, if only Mrs Rindfuss wouldn't find her note in the book, Emily thought. If only it could fall out now without her seeing it. No chance of that – she had the book in an iron grip.

'You're under arrest, Book,' Gary said in a loud whisper when she had gone. Everyone laughed but Emily.

Oh, *you* can joke, she thought miserably as she tried to keep her mind on her homework. But every time she thought about what had happened, she broke her pencil.

What would Mrs Rindfuss do if she found the note? Would she be angry? Emily tried to remember what she had written in it. Just something about Captain Robodek, she thought. She hadn't signed her name, so no one could know for sure who it was.

Another thought occurred to her. Suppose Mrs Rindfuss read the note *out loud* to *everyone*? She broke her pencil again.

But the worst part was that she and Cosmic Cousin could never leave books under the table again. How was she going to discover who Cosmic Cousin was? Emily's spirits sank lower and lower.

It was almost time to leave. Emily decided to make one last attempt. She was taking a big risk, but she had to get in touch with Cosmic Cousin. She'd leave one more note under the table and hope Mrs Rindfuss didn't find it. And just in case Cosmic Cousin hadn't been there when the ledge was discovered, she would leave a warning that their hiding place wasn't safe any more.

Dear Cosmic Cousin,

We can't leave books here anymore since you-know-who is on to it. Please let me know who you are. I can't tell you my name in case you-know-who finds this note. Wear something red on Thursday when you come to the library, and I'll do the same.

Your Solar Soulmate

Emily hesitated a long time over the 'something red' idea, but she couldn't think of anything better. Thursday was two days off. That should give Cosmic Cousin time to find the note. But if Mrs Rindfuss found it first, she'd be sure to spot Emily in her red anorak. (Or rather, in Alma's red anorak that Emily was planning to borrow.) She would have to take that chance.

Emily waited till almost everyone had gone home. Then she left the note, folded up small, on the ledge under the table.

10

Cosmic Surprise

It was Thursday, after school, and
Emily was standing just inside the door
of the library, watching the kids coming
in. All day she had spotted kids in red –
red shirts, red sweaters, red backpacks.
Now where were they?

Maybe Cosmic Cousin would put on
something red at the last minute. Emily
wished she had thought of doing that
instead of borrowing Alma's hot, bulky
anorak. She could have kept her red
spaceship pin in her pocket and put it
on now.

Checking something small, she
looked at hair ribbons, belts, shoes,
socks. . . Hey! Walter Kenney was

wearing red socks. She never should have crossed Walter off her list.

Emily walked quickly over to Walter's table. There was no place to sit down so she stood next to his chair.

'Hi, Walter.' She zipped the zipper of her anorak up and down very fast. Although Walter looked up and gave her a big smile, it wasn't a so-you're-Solar-Soulmate smile. Emily stood there for a few more moments, zipping more slowly and feeling silly. Walter didn't look up again but everyone at his table did.

'Sorry, no seats left. Why don't you *zip* on over to another table?' Eddie said. He was still laughing at his own joke as Emily hurried away. Her face was as red as her jacket.

She sat down at the table by the window and took out her books. She'd be more careful the next time, she thought, and not fall for a stupid little patch of red like that. She tried to think about homework.

Suddenly she caught a flash of red out of the corner of her eye. Janie Hines had just walked in with a red scarf around her neck.

Janie Hines? Why hadn't she thought of her before? After all, Janie was a good friend of Rachel's. And Rachel was the one who had got Emily interested in outer space. Maybe Janie had picked up the same interest from Rachel.

Janie was just the sort of person Emily wanted Cosmic Cousin to be. She was fun to talk to. She had a great sense of humour. And she lived only two blocks away from her. Emily was getting more excited by the minute. She stood up to get Janie's attention.

Then Janie took off the scarf and

stuffed it into her pocket. Cosmic Cousin wouldn't do that. Emily pretended she had needed to stretch and then sat down again. She felt completely let down now. Janie would have been a perfect Cosmic Cousin.

Looking around, she couldn't see any more red, and she began to have dark thoughts. Maybe Cosmic Cousin had never found her note. She checked the table ledge. The note was gone, but what did that mean? Since nobody was wearing red, it must mean Mrs Rindfuss had found the note. She would have noticed Emily in the red anorak. When she checked out books, Mrs Rindfuss would point a long bony finger at her and say, 'I always knew you were a troublemaker, Emily Butler.'

Emily decided not to check out any books that day.

Without Cosmic Cousin to look
forward to, time passed as slowly as at
school. No one new came into the
library. The only excitement was when
Stanley knocked over the Hallowe'en
book display. Marcie and Mary Louise

helped him pick up the books. Mrs Rindfuss blamed all three of them, so Emily was glad she hadn't helped.

It was almost closing time now, and nearly everyone had gone but Emily. She was afraid to go past the desk.

Mrs Rindfuss walked over to Emily's table and cleared her throat loudly. Here it comes, thought Emily.

'You had better hurry if you have any books to check out,' Mrs Rindfuss said. 'Both of you must have big stacks, as usual. Two of a kind, I'd say.'

Two of a kind? Emily looked up. Mary Louise and she were the only ones left.

'By the way, Mary Louise, here's that book you were asking for the other day. It's no wonder you couldn't find it. Someone had *hidden* it.' Mrs Rindfuss gave Emily a sharp glance. She handed *Intergalactic Mutiny* to Mary Louise and went back to her desk.

Emily sat very still and stared at Mary Louise. Mary Louise was looking down, slowly picking up her books.

'*You're* Cosmic Cousin!' Emily said at last.

Oh, no! It just couldn't be. She raced quickly through everything she knew about Mary Louise. Of course, Mary Louise did go to her school and she did study at the library, but Emily had never considered her. She had thought that Cosmic Cousin would be someone more . . . exciting. Someone like Janie Hines.

Now that she knew, she almost wished she could go back to not knowing.

Mary Louise still didn't look up but she said in a low voice, 'I found your note – about not leaving any more books under the table.'

'But you're not wearing anything

red,' Emily protested. There had to be some mistake. She didn't want it to be *Mary Louise Butterman*.

Then Mary Louise pulled up her sleeve so Emily could see her watch. The band was bright red, all the

numbers were in red, and there was a
ladybird in the centre. 'It's not very big
but I don't have anything else that's
red,' she said, looking down at her feet.
'I was going to show you my watch at
school today. . .'

'That means you already knew I was
Solar Soulmate,' Emily said accusingly.

'Yes. I knew when you gave your
book report on *Terrors of the Time
Warp*. That was one of the first books I
left a note in.'

'What book did you do your report
on?' Emily asked.

'*Trapped in the Asteroid Belt*.'

'But I never heard it,' Emily said.
And then she remembered. She had
been home with the flu the day Mary
Louise gave her book report.

Emily thought of something else.
'Why weren't those notes in your
handwriting?'

'Oh, I've been practising a new way lately. I like the way Eddie writes. Have you ever noticed his handwriting?'

Emily nodded grimly.

'I think it looks nice. Sort of elegant,' Mary Louise added.

They were silent for a moment.

'Why did you start leaving those notes in the first place?' Emily asked.

'I got the idea from *Pioneer 10*,' Mary Louise said.

'What's that?'

'It's a spacecraft they sent into outer space with a message from Earth. Maybe somebody in another solar system – away on the other side of the universe – will find the message. I like that idea. It's sort of like sending a note in a bottle.' Now Mary Louise was looking right at her as she talked. Emily had never heard her say so much. 'My friend Sonia told me about it. She's always reading about science and space.'

Emily felt a twinge of jealousy. 'You're lucky . . . having a friend like that.'

Mary Louise looked a little sad. 'She was my best friend before we moved. I guess that's why I started leaving notes. I wanted to find someone who likes the things I do.'

'Then *why* didn't you tell me who you were?' Emily burst out.

'I thought if I kept it a secret, we could be friends – sort of. I wasn't sure you would want to know it was me,' Mary Louise said.

Emily winced at that. It was too near the truth.

'Girls!' The lights flashed off and on.

Emily and Mary Louise grabbed their books and walked to the desk. Mrs Rindfuss was waiting for them, tapping

her foot. 'Here it is, after closing time,' she grumbled as she checked out Mary Louise's books. 'It would have to be you two. How many times do I have to remind you of the library rule: Books must be brought to the desk fifteen minutes before closing time.'

After Mrs Rindfuss had shooed them through the door, they lingered on the steps for a few minutes.

'I should have left earlier,' Mary Louise said. 'I wanted to finish my Hallowe'en costume tonight.'

Emily remembered what Marcie had said. 'Your fairy princess costume?'

Mary Louise looked surprised. 'Fairy princess? No. My comet costume. I have to glue more sequins on the tail part.'

'A comet! Wow!' Now that seemed more like Cosmic Cousin.

'Could you help me finish my UFO costume?' Emily asked.

'Sure.'

Emily was feeling happier by the minute. 'Have you ever made a map of the constellations?' she asked.

'I started one last summer,' Mary Louise answered.

They could hear Mrs Rindfuss locking the front door. 'Isn't it time for you girls to be going home?' she said as she passed them.

After she was gone, Emily looked at Mary Louise and asked, 'Who does she remind you of?'

'Mrs Rindfuss?' Mary Louise thought for a moment. 'The Martian Zyvitch?'

'Right.' Emily grinned. Only Cosmic Cousin would have known that.